# Disney's
## My Very First Winnie the Pooh™

# Pooh's Favorite
# Things About Spring

Written by
## Kathleen W. Zoehfeld

Illustrated by
## Robbin Cuddy

SCHOLASTIC INC.

New York  Toronto  London  Auckland  Sydney
Mexico City  New Delhi  Hong Kong  Buenos Aires

First published by Disney Press, New York, NY.
This edition published by Scholastic Inc., 90 Old Sherman Turnpike, Danbury, CT 06816
by arrangement with Disney Licensed Publishing.

SCHOLASTIC and associated logos are trademarks
and/or registered trademarks of Scholastic Inc.

ISBN 0-7172-6411-4

Printed in the U.S.A.

One morning Winnie the Pooh woke up to the sound of icicles melting, *drip, drip, drip.* He rubbed his sleepy eyes and felt sunshine pouring through his window like warm honey.

Time for a little something, he decided happily.

Pooh went to his cupboard to find his breakfast.
"Oh, bother," he said. His honeypots were empty.

"Cheer-up, cheerily, cheer-up, cheerily," sang a
robin outside Pooh's window.

"Buzz, buzz, buzzzz," sang a honeybee.

Pooh began to feel like singing, too.

*I think the spring is springing.*
*I can hear the robin singing,*
*And the icicles are melting—*
*Drip, drip, drip.*
*So I'm following the buzzing bee,*
*Skipping to the honey tree!*

Pooh took a honeypot and went out into the fine warm morning. He skipped through the soft grass, up the path toward the honey tree.

When he reached the bridge, he rested for a bit to watch the river racing underneath. Up above, little clouds were playing in the bright sky. And all around him the forest trees were putting on their new green lace.

"Hello, Pooh Bear!" called Rabbit. "No time for sitting! It's springtime—time to get the garden planted." Rabbit hurried past with a wheelbarrow full of tools and seeds.

"Oh," said Pooh. Then the rumble of his own tummy made him remember breakfast. No time for sitting, he thought.

Pooh picked up his honeypot and walked through the meadow, all bright with flowers. And he sang a little more of his song.

> *Oh, the big river's racing,*
> *And the beech trees are lacing.*
> *Spring is really springing,*
> *All around.*
> *So I'm following the buzzing bee,*
> *Skipping to the honey tree.*

Before he knew it, Pooh had reached the place where the stepping stones went across the stream. One, two, three he stepped. But, at the third stone, the sun felt so warm that he decided to have a little sit.

He listened to the creek bubbling and to the spring peepers chirping. He watched a baby turtle and four bugs crawling along the rocks.

"Hello, Pooh!" called Owl, flying overhead. "Isn't it a glorious day! I'm off to do my spring cleaning. No time for sitting—time to feather the nest!"

"Good-bye, Owl," said Pooh. And once again his tummy reminded him that he hadn't had any breakfast. No time for sitting, he thought.

Pooh picked up his honeypot and strolled through the green and mossy woods. And he sang:

*I hear the peepers peeping,*
*But the shiny beetles creeping*
*Are as quiet as the violets*
*In the breeze.*
*So I'm following the buzzing bee,*
*Skipping to the honey tree.*

As soon as he came out of the woods, Pooh thought about how good it would feel to rest again. He sat in the new grass. He smelled the green smells and counted five yellow buttercups.

"Hello, Pooh," said Eeyore. "I believe you're sitting on some of my thistles. Spring thistles are much better when they are not sat upon by bears."

"Ow!" said Pooh. "And bears are much better when they don't sit upon thistles."

The thistles reminded Pooh that he still had not had any breakfast. "No time for sitting," he said, plucking a pricker from behind him.

As Eeyore piled up his thistles, Pooh picked up his honeypot and skipped up the hill toward the honey tree.

*I feel the thistles prickling,*
*And the green, green grass is tickling*
*My feet.*
*That's how I know the spring is springing,*
*And that's why Pooh is singing—*
*Following the buzzing bee*
*Skipping to the honey tree.*

"Follow the buzzing bee!" cried Pooh, as he climbed the honey tree and reached into the hollow. He took one, two, three pawfuls of honey. Then he filled his pot. Then he licked the pot clean and filled it again. After the third pot, Pooh began to think a picnic sounded like a very nice thing.

"But my friends are all busy with their spring chores." Pooh sighed. "I wonder what they'll think."

To his surprise, everyone agreed that a picnic was a splendid idea.

They gathered at the picnic spot, and Kanga spread out the blanket. She paused to watch as a mama duck passed with her six fluffy ducklings waddling behind. "Aren't they little dears," Kanga said. She tucked Roo in her pouch and patted him gently.

Piglet took haycorn pies and honeypots out of a large basket. And Eeyore laid out plenty of tender thistles.

Everyone sat around the picnic blanket and smiled and laughed in the sun.

"Ahhhh," said Pooh happily. "Maybe spring *is* a good time for sitting."

"Pooh," cried Rabbit, "you're absolutely right! Spring is a busy time. But I think the best thing about spring is sitting and listening to the robins singing . . ."

"And watching the bluebells ringing," added Tigger.

"And smelling the brown earth greening," chimed Roo.

"And feeling all warm and sunny," sighed Piglet.
And tasting pots of honey!" cried Pooh.